Big Bad Raps

To Edna Blake and her class of 1993-4
at King Hedges School, Cambridge
T.M.

ORCHARD BOOKS
338 Euston Road,
London NW1 3BH
Orchard Books Australia
Hachette Children's Books
Level 17/207 Kent Street, Sydney, NSW 2000
First published in Great Britain in 1996
First paperback publication in 1997
This edition published in 2004

A CIP catalogue record for this books is available from the British library.
978 1 84362 751 7
5 7 9 10 8 6 4
Printed in Great Britain

Tony Mitton

Illustrated by Martin Chatterton

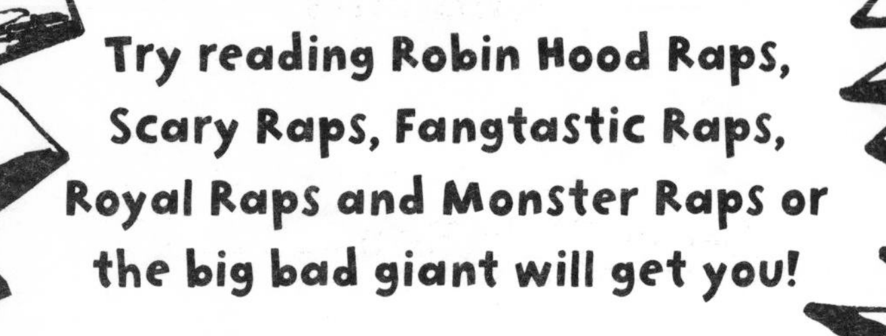
Try reading Robin Hood Raps,
Scary Raps, Fangtastic Raps,
Royal Raps and Monster Raps or
the big bad giant will get you!

Contents

Beans Talk Rap

Did you ever hear tell
of brave young Jack?
He lived with his mother
in a tumbledown shack.
They had no money
and they had no bread,
and things looked bad
so his old ma said,

So Jack got up
with a yawn and a frown.
Then he took old Daisy
and he went to town.

But as he went truckin'
on down the road
he heard a voice say,
"I'll be blowed!
That's just the kind
of cow I need.
I'll take her now,
why, yes indeed!

I'm happy to pay
and I sure ain't mean.
So give me five,
here's a magic bean."
Well, the man looked weird,
kind of old and wise,
with a crazy hat
and big green eyes.

And Jack thought,

This here's a
magic dude.
This bean means
money and plenty
of food

The man took the cow.
Jack took the bean.

Let's cut here now
and change the scene:

“You beanhead, Jack!”
his old ma said.
“What use is this?
Oh, go to bed!”

And she threw that bean
way out in the yard.
Then she went to bed
and she cried so hard.

But when she woke
the very next day,
she didn't know what
to think or say...
for a beanstalk grew
way up in the sky,
'bout three feet thick
and a hundred high!

"Now, don't you worry
a thing about me.
I'll see you soon, Ma.
Back for tea."
Those were the words
that brave Jack said
as he put on his boots.
Then up he sped.

When he got to the top
way above the cloud,
he could hear a voice
that boomed out loud.
The voice said, "Fee!"
and the voice said, "Fi!
I am the giant
who lives in the sky."
And a sign read:

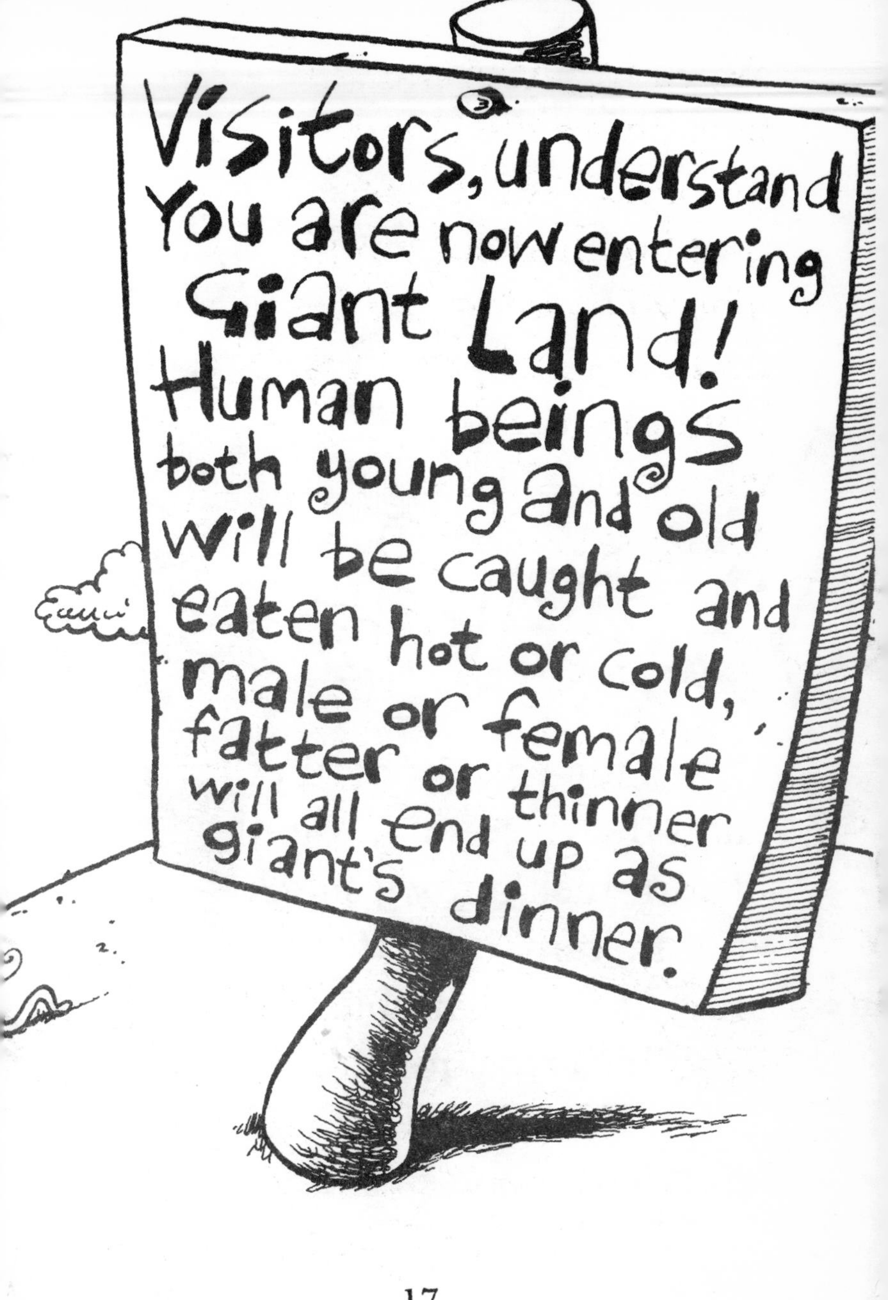

Visitors, understand
You are now entering
Giant Land!
Human beings
both young and old
will be caught and
eaten hot or cold,
male or female
fatter or thinner
will all end up as
giant's dinner.

Then the voice said, "Fo!"
and the voice said, "Fum!
I can smell a tasty snack
for my tum."
But Jack was nimble
and Jack was quick.
With his young good looks
and his tongue so slick

he was quite a hit
with the giant's wife,
so she hid him away
and saved his life.
Then bit by bit
he took his chance
and he led that giant
a mean old dance.

He took his guitar
and he took his gold.

That boy was quick
and he sure was bold.
Then he hid behind
a table leg
and he stole the goose
with the golden egg.

The goose gave a cackle,

So the giant woke up
with a mighty shout.
"Say, cut that cackle, Goose,"
said Jack,
"or I'll end up served
as a tea-time snack."

He slid down the stalk
as quick as he could
and he got him an axe
for chopping wood.
Jack chopped fast.
The giant gave a cry!
Then he tumbled down
from the deep blue sky.

He hit the earth
and he went clean through
till he came to the land
of the kangaroo.
The hole closed up
and he never came back.
"That was a near one.
Phew!" breathed Jack.

"Hey, Ma!" he called.
"Come out and see.
I told you I'd be back
for tea."
"What's this?" shrieked Ma.
"It's ours," smiled Jack.
And from that time
they've never looked back.

Fol de Rol Rap

Well, the Billy-Goats Three,
they were nibbling away,
when the little one stopped
and began to say,
"Just look at that grass
so sweet and green.
It's the juiciest grass
I've ever seen."

Now to get to that grass
they had to cross a river.
But listen to this
(It'll make you shiver):
Under the bridge
there lived a troll,
and what he sang
was, "Fol de rol!"

"If one of those billy-goats
passes by
they'll end up baked
in a Billy-Goat Pie."
Then along came the little one,
clickety-clack.
"Oh ho!" said the troll,

But the little one said,

But the middle one said,

So the dumb old troll,
he licked his lips
and stood and waited,
hands on hips.
But the Big Bill said,

and he gave that troll
a billy-goat punch.

The troll went SPLASH!
and he looked quite ill
as the river rushed him
down the hill.
And the last I heard
he was far away,
living on slugs
and snails and hay.

But high on the hill
those Billy-Goats Three
are eating the greenest
grass for tea.

And that's the end
of this story.

Huff-Puff Houses

Huff-puff houses
are made of straw.

They end up flat
on the forest floor.

Huff-puff houses
are made of sticks.

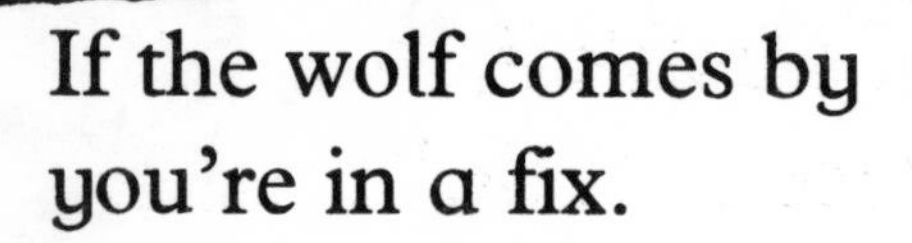

If the wolf comes by
you're in a fix.

So make your house
of bricks and mortar.
And put on a pot
of boiling water.
Then if the wolf
comes trying his luck,
say "Sorry, Mr Wolf,
my front door's stuck."

"But, oh by the hairs
on my chinny chin chin,
the chimney's open
so do drop in."
And if he tries
I'll guarantee
that mean old wolf
won't stay for tea.

Or if he does,
then you and I
will both sit down
to Hot Wolf Pie!

(And if that don't
agree with you
we'll turn it into
Big Wolf Stew.)

Little Red Rap

Just on the edge
of a deep, dark wood
lived a girl called
Little Red Riding Hood.
Her grandmother lived
not far away,
so Red went to pay her
a visit one day.

She took some cake
and she took some wine
packed up in a basket
nice and fine.

And her ma said, "Red,
now just watch out,
for they say that
Big Bad Wolf's about."

But Red went off
with a hop and a skip.
She was feeling good,
she was feeling hip.
So she took her time,
she picked some flowers,
and soon the minutes
had grown to hours.

And the Big Bad Wolf,
who knew her plan,
he turned his nose
and he ran and ran.
He ran till he came
to her grandmother's door.
Then he locked her up
with a great big roar.

He took her place
in her nice warm bed,
and he waited there
for Little Miss Red.
So when Little Red,
she stepped inside,
that wolf, his eyes
went open wide.

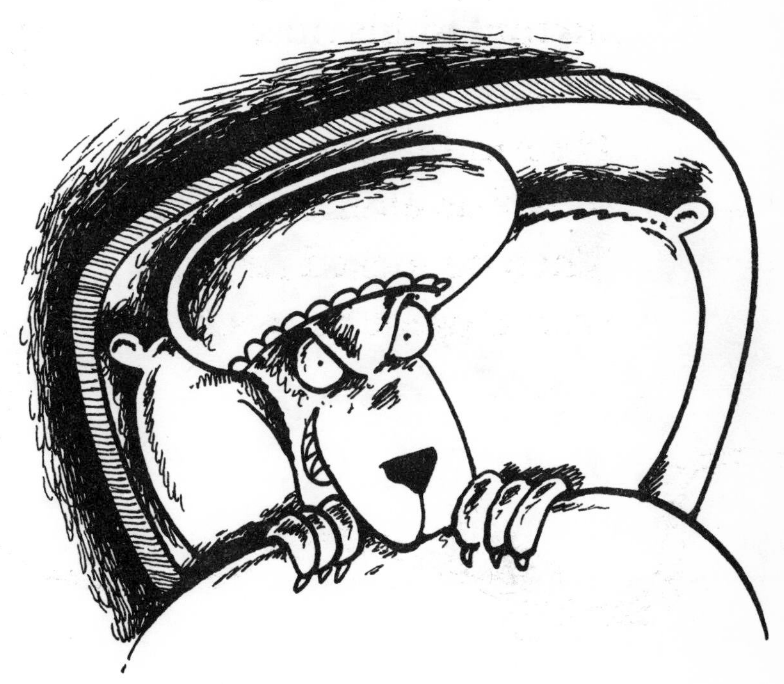

Says Red, "Why, Gran,
what great big eyes!"
Says Wolf, "I'm trying
you out for size."

Says Red, "Why, Gran,
you're covered in hair!"
Says Wolf, "Now, dear,
it's rude to stare."

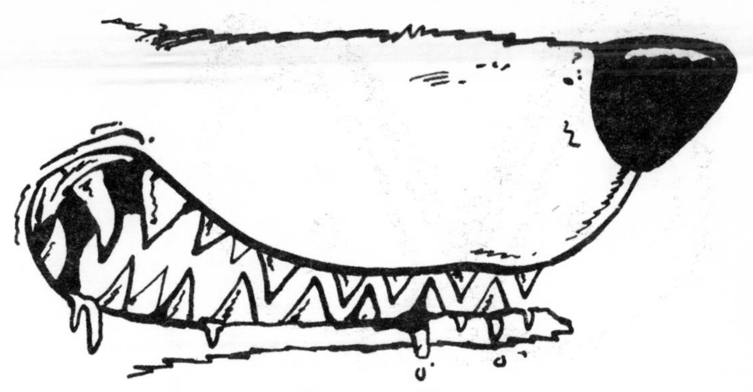

Says Red, "Why, Gran,
what great big claws,
what great big teeth,
what great big jaws!

And goodness, Gran,
what a great big grin!"
Says Wolf, "All the better
to fit you in!"

But Little Miss Red
says, "Not so fast..."
and she calls to a woodcutter
strolling past.
"Hey, you there, John!
Can I borrow your axe?"
And she gave that Wolfie
three good whacks.

"That's one from Gran
and one from me
and one delivered
entirely free."

That wolf ran off
with a holler and a shout
and Little Miss Red
let Grandma out.

They called the woodcutter
in to dine
and they all sat down
to the cake and the wine.

And that's how the story ends –
Just fine!